Aurora Presents
Don Bluth Productions'

The Secret of NIMH

MRS. BRISBY
and the Magic Stone

ADAPTED BY GINA INGOGLIA
ILLUSTRATED BY CAROL NICKLAUS

Illustrations are based on the original art from Don Bluth Productions' film THE SECRET OF NIMH.
The film THE SECRET OF NIMH is based upon the book MRS. FRISBY AND THE RATS OF NIMH by Robert C. O'Brien.

A GOLDEN BOOK · NEW YORK
Western Publishing Company, Inc., Racine, Wisconsin 53404

Mrs. Brisby was getting ready to go out. She kissed her children good-by, then glanced in the mirror.

"My," she thought, "the red stone the rats gave me looks extra sparkly today!"

She hurried across the field.
"There's not much time," she said to herself. "The farmer will start plowing tomorrow, and my house is right in his path! Thank goodness the rats are going to move it to a safe spot."

    Near the rosebush one of the rats came out to
meet her.

    "I'm so glad to see you, Justin," said Mrs. Brisby.
"Thank you for helping us."

    Justin smiled. "Your husband, Jonathan, was a very
brave mouse and a great friend of the rats. We would
do anything for his family."

"You're pretty brave yourself," said Justin as they walked to the farmhouse. "After all, you offered to put the sleeping powder in the cat's food. We could never move your house with the cat awake."

"But I feel so frightened now," said Mrs. Brisby.
"You are braver than you think," said Justin. "And that stone we gave you has magic powers when it is worn by one with a courageous heart. When it glows, you can do anything."

Justin and Mrs. Brisby peeked up through a hole in the farmhouse floor.

"The cat's under the table," whispered Justin. He gave Mrs. Brisby a packet. "Sprinkle this in his bowl. And be careful! You'd better leave your cape and necklace here—they might get caught on something."

Mrs. Brisby crawled through the hole and dashed across the room. She shivered as she thought of the cat's sharp teeth and long claws.

At last she reached the bowl. She quickly shook the powder into the cat's food, then darted toward the door.

Suddenly a metal colander came down over her.
"Look, Mom," said a boy's voice. "I caught a mouse!
I'm going to keep it as a pet."
The boy locked Mrs. Brisby in a birdcage.

Justin saw everything. He ran to tell the other rats what had happened.

"We'll have to work even faster now," he said. "We must move the house *and* try to rescue Mrs. Brisby before the cat wakes up."

Just as he finished speaking, there was a loud clap of thunder.

It began to rain, but that did not stop the rats. They tied long ropes around Mrs. Brisby's house and, with pulleys, began hoisting it in the air.

The rats pulled and strained at the ropes. The house was heavier than they thought.

Suddenly, with a *snap*, the ropes broke.

Mrs. Brisby's house went splashing into the mud.

  In the farmhouse, Mrs. Brisby was trying to find a
way out of the cage.
  "I should be helping Justin and the others," she
thought. "And my children need me!"
  All at once she spotted a tiny opening at the other
side of the water feeder.

Holding her breath, Mrs. Brisby dove into
the water, swam across, and squeezed through
the opening.

She stood at the edge of the birdcage and looked
down. There, asleep on the floor, was the cat.

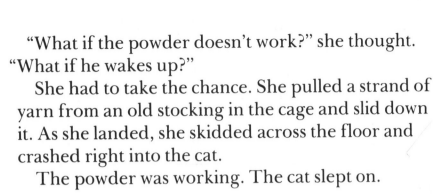

"What if the powder doesn't work?" she thought. "What if he wakes up?"

She had to take the chance. She pulled a strand of yarn from an old stocking in the cage and slid down it. As she landed, she skidded across the floor and crashed right into the cat.

The powder was working. The cat slept on.

Mrs. Brisby crawled back through the hole in the floor, picked up her cape and necklace, and raced across the field to where the rats were working.

"What happened?" she cried when she saw her house sinking in the mud.

"The ropes broke," said Justin. "But we're working as fast as we can to set up a new rig."

Frightened voices came from inside the house.
"The mud's coming in everywhere!" Mrs. Brisby's
children cried. "Help us, Mommy!"

"I have to save my children," said Mrs. Brisby. "If the stone has magic powers, it will help me now."

She leaped to the top of her sinking house. As the mud came up around her feet, the stone began to glow.

"Mrs. Brisby, come back before you sink, too!" cried Justin, pulling her out of the mud.

But Mrs. Brisby was thinking only of her children. The stone was fiery red now.

As if by magic, the house began to rise. Higher and higher it went, until it was completely out of the mud. Then it floated across the field until it was nestled safely next to a big rock.

As her children gathered around her, Mrs. Brisby gave Justin the red stone. "I won't be needing this any more," she said. "But perhaps someday you will. You were right—it really is magic."

"And you really are brave," said Justin. "You proved that today."

Mrs. Brisby smiled and drew her children closer. "Brave deeds are not so hard when you do them for the ones you love," she said.